Hurry Up, Gus!

Written by

Derek L. Polen

Goal Line Group LLC

ISBN-13: 978-1-7335651-3-4 (Paperback)
ISBN-13: 978-1-7335651-2-7 (Hardcover)

Illustrations drawn with pencil and digitally painted by artist Lesta Ginting.

Thanks to my Mom for giving me the idea
that led to this book!

Today is a big day for Gus. It is the day of his first school track meet. Gus stayed up late playing video games instead of going to sleep when his mom told him to. He was tired and did not want to get out of bed. Gus was already off to a slow start.

He finally got out of bed when he

heard his mother say,

"You are going to miss breakfast

if you do not hurry up, Gus."

While eating breakfast his Mom looked

out the window, saw the bus

coming down the road and said,

"Gus, hurry up or you will miss the bus!"

Gus ate two bites of toast, grabbed his backpack, and dashed out the door. His brother was already at the bus and yelled, "Hurry up, Gus, or you will be late for school!"

As he sat quietly reading in his first class, his stomach started growling loudly. Everyone heard it and started laughing. Gus got embarrassed and thought to himself,

"If only I hurried up this morning getting ready, I would have been able to eat my breakfast."

Before his next class he saw some friends in the hallway. They started talking about the big track meet after school.

Gus was so busy talking to his friends that he was late for Math class. His teacher, Mr. Squareroot, said, "Gus, you are late again. Come see me after school."

As the school day came to an end, Gus went back to Mr. Squareroot's class.

As Mr. Squareroot was meeting with the Math Club, he made Gus write out sentences saying he would arrive to class on time.

will arrive to class on time.
will arrive to class on time.
will arrive to Class on time.
I will arrive

When Gus finished writing his sentences he rushed off to the track meet. Just as Gus arrived at the starting line the race kicked off! Gus ran as fast as he could, but finished in last place.

Gus went home thinking about what a bummer his day was. He was late for everything. He missed breakfast, got embarrassed, was late for class, and came in last at the track meet.

Gus decided that tomorrow he would turn things around so he did not have to hurry up all the time.

The next day, Gus got up when the alarm clock went off and got ready on time. He ate all of his breakfast and made it to the school bus without being rushed.
Gus was off to a great start!

Gus was able to pay attention in class, since he was not distracted by being hungry. When it was time to go to Mr. Squareroot's class he watched the clock and told his friends,

"I have to get to class."

Today was another track meet for Gus. When school ended, he got ready and arrived at the meet on time.

When the race started, Gus was in the lead. The coach yelled, "Hurry up, Gus, the others are closing in!" Gus hurried and won a first place victory.

After the race, Gus went to Galactic Goodies with his Mom to celebrate. As Gus quickly started to eat his ice cream, his Mom leaned over and said, "Let's just enjoy our ice cream, Gus. There is no need to hurry up now."

The End

For your next books, check out:

Max was the biggest dinosaur fan in Fossil Lake. He enjoyed playing in his toy dinosaur city, studying dinosaurs at the museum, and digging for fossils. One day, while digging at the fossil park, Max believes he discovers a dinosaur in the sky. Will Max discover a dinosaur or some other amazing creature?

Andy and Grace are moving to Bigcityopolis and getting ready to go on a new adventure. Unsure at first, Andy and Grace learn to realize that moving to Bigcityopolis can be fun and full of interesting things to do. This story encourages children to be curious about transitioning to a new city or school. As with any new change, it might just turn out to be an amazing adventure!

CPSIA information can be obtained
at www.ICGtesting.com
Printed in the USA
LVHW071452141119
637369LV00005B/34/P